NEON LINE

TOM THOMPSON

ETT IMPRINT

Exile Bay

This edition published by ETT Imprint, Exile Bay in 2022

First published by Second Back Row Press in 1978

First electronic edition ETT Imprint 2022

ETT Imprint,
PO Box 1906,
Royal Exchange NSW 1225
Australia

ISBN   978-1-922698-15-5 (pbk)
ISBN   978-1-922698-16-2 (ebk)

Cover: Photograph by Russell Workman shows William Street towards Kings Cross inthe early 1970s.

NEON LINE

Acknowledgements

That island
floating in the sea,
just as the street-lights
come on

Charles Olsen

THE
ENTICER

THE ENTICER

SYDNEY (Hebrew) : 'The Enticer' (Feminine)

He'd dreamt of this place for years & never been here.

Now at last living in it, no more country towns.

Walking along grey-slate lanes wet with rain, taxi-tyres lurching above the Harbour Bridge — She says that there's a mist hanging over this drunken night. It's the beginning of a new year, their first year in the City. Both stare at the bridge coupling two dark coasts spot-lit. Marlene annoyed says 'Let's eat fish,' so they turn toward the Sorrento Cafe; over lanes of sliding traffic . . .

At the Sorrento finding their way blocked by lazy Greek hands, strong-armed aprons saying 'Bye bye buddy.'

Views from a taxi to Hyde Park, Sydney cold & grey. "My Lost City is drowning ..." Laughing with couples under street light they drink to the rebellion of Lost Youth, fragmented adolescence under pressure. Like bona-fide travellers they talk with the recklessness of a past frustrated life; trying to fix a damp fuse, restore electricity to ElectriCity.

From the country the City glows. Through Paddington . . .
Smell the smell of sweet Continental breads —

Long grey-black lanes streaked with yellow, red spots blinking in the shadows of terraces. "Why so many Italian children in the streets this late at night?" Loose-wrought iron barricades. Warped small triangular parks & tenements. Some half-slung attempts at restoration, undressed Bakeries, home-made chocolates & Salami joints meet trees hinged to belted walkways. Dead trees in allotments, vacant allotment blocks . . . Stumbling through long harbour nights, night lights —

In town Museum drowns in the heavy deluge. Midgets skate the streets under gaudy red umbrellas selling headlines, vanish. George Street the colour of damp sand. Pitt Street, of grey crumpled stone, soft cardboard. Peering into the People's Palace — Juveniles with leaping haircuts, peanut shells over crusty carpets . . .

Trying to get drunk on a Saturday night. She's wearing sky-blue silk turning blue-black. So bruised & upset, just wanting to sit down, "maybe at the movies ..."

Outside the Golbourn Club they sing nostalgias by the Drifters & the Flamingoes, thinking that Poker & Fats Domino makes the night-life enticing —

'This must be, the Life!' says Marlene.

'Oh yes M, yes.'

Cold shoes, walking through a field of sky-scrapers. She says "I wanna go home." Lights blinking off in sections all over town — its deserted streets evaporating: Lunar walks, its incantations, incantating — the ways & walk-talk sneers of young Continental girls. Walking home through tenements, sleet-grey; warehouses empty on wet streets. In this greyness — "This City is dead."

They try to flee the City, groping / homeward.

They hit the station. Central. Marlene shaking, "No." Wet & blue she wants to stay roasting in the arms of the Century & the Southern Cross Hotels . . . Sam adrift on greasy Central Railway, under the warmth of steaming roticeries this old aircraft hangar balloons above him. Blue uniformed attendants, "Hey now wait a second you got a ticket?" Fastening his hands to the wooden seat.

Ahead, long whistling night, & phosphorescent stations. . .

Going over the Bridge, Hell Gate, bright lights burning up the Quay. With 'the Enticer', high overlooking — the limits & the ends black in webs of oilslick water. Shining, every theme recurs in bizarre entangled light — clash of Harbour Bridge line Luna madness — Falling towards the din, "Sweet Jesus M, what have I dreamt ...

MARLENE DIETRICH IN THE BATHROOM

MARLENE DIETRICH
IN THE BATHROOM

Oh those terrible years, when you had to be somebody,
or make somebody up.

Marlene at the kitchen sink watching water swirl, go down the stainless steel line outside her flat. In an ice-silk night dress it is twelve o'clock under a single globe. Her belly turns protruding. 'Let me show you photographs,' she says. Her child wakes hoarse-wailing in the next room.

Marlene, her dress open at the arms; arms high with photographs shows the white flesh of her breasts. Light reddish-brown hair. She puts them down to open a black box, hair covering her eyes. Sam pours the claret as baby wanders in.

Marlene looks around her suddenly lost. Arms high. 'Look!' Sam stares intently at the photographs — Young Scottish maniacs with Hugh McDarmiad beards and wisp-thin lips. Marlene smiles, unburdening . . .

'All these were My Man at one time or another. All strikingly the same beauty. All but the baby's father here. Of him I've lost the pictures. Got the baby, not the father — ' She laughs, baby sniffling fingers over her lilac gown, dabbing fingers on the silk.

'Crazy,' she says, posturing, 'There are hundreds of me!' Her eager hands tear cardboard to reveal 8 by 10's, black, glossy, spilling over raw floor. Feint harbour breeze . . . through the window. Her picture world exposed — Marlene semi-clothed, naked; fear over slight white breasts. Shimmering black and white. 'The Blonde Venus, ' she says, 'How come I never got the job?'

She passes more olives and cheese. Marlene talking fitful-lap-sleep with child. Marlene talking French. Sam pours the claret, not understanding. Suddenly she holds his head, eye-to-eye kissing him with eyes open. Luring filmicly. Sam stirs disheartened at the table, — 'What about Vaughn asleep next door?' Marlene shakes her head, hair — 'I'm the daughter of the Movies,' she says.

Marlene lilac under yellow globe, her silk belly swaying electric light. Drinking wine to ease her anger over flat rents and vague jobs. No money, debts. Her sick child breathing slowly . . . She smiles, 'Remember Dietrich in the Blue Angel?'

Sam nods, nearly remembering. Waiting, looks up — Marlene stares into her window-reflection, at the half-drawn lines. Face white, over-exposed. She gives Sam the baby and leaves the photo floor.

Sam carries the child from the kitchen listening to the water, sink-flow, leaving the flat. He stands at the bathroom door — Marlene is at the mirror, her face —in photographs— reflected, make-up over silk gown. One breast swaying, dirty feet.

On her right hand, her reflected left; a window over tiny bathtub brays humming from the freighter yards, Balmain wharves. Ships from every corner of the globe —New York, Paris— passing across her window face.

'Morroco!' she says. 'Made in 1932.' Sam checks the ships . . .

In the harbour, water running down from the sink. Sam leaves the room.

Marlene is somewhere in the ocean . . .

FREEWHEELING

FREEWHEELING

There are two people on a mountain road, coming towards each other. The woman is walking downhill while the man struggles with a bicycle. Snaking his way towards her, the hot dry sand squeezes together then out under the tyres. Legs push down into the revolving wheels. He dismounts and walks directly to the woman.

The picture becomes clearer.

The woman is young and slim and holds her body like a man's. She stares at his brown face and wiry frame. At the green bicycle —

He says, 'Hello . . . ' Coiled, intense.

Leaning on his bicycle he gives her his address, close to her own destination. She walks on, feeling ill. Down the road towards his house, over tyre-tracks sliding underneath her . . . All around her the landscape tumbles and groans —

She doesn't turn around.

With her friends around a kitchen table, endless cups of tea. Talk of their 'husbands', deserted or thrown out, of necessity. Marlene tells them about the cyclist.

'You mean you talked?'

She let them ramble on about the other men they knew of, exactly like that.

Marlene wakes up in the middle of the night imagining his blue eyes. The man sleeping next to her still snores. Blue will get up in the morning and go to work.

She tries to see the cyclist, walking across the firetrail through the bush.

He stands in his garden drying his hands on the fence. Resting his arm next to hers they talk animated. She tells him about the other women. About their fears of him. He laughs and shows her a letter from the Council asking him to leave . . .

'It's just talk,' he says.

'They're crazy women . . . '

'I'll stay silent.'

'That's what they hate you for —'

'I give them neither flattery or ammunition.'

'Just a flattening.'

'I'm immune —'

They laugh, unwinding. Their bodies quicken in the sun under sheets of thin stress.

'Thank you for taking care of me this way,' he says.

At home with Blue she acts in half-daze, she can't respond. It's too much effort and her mind is miles away . . . She kisses him blankly on the mouth.

Night : Through the webbing of fruit trees she sees the street light thirty yards away. The road curves . . . She feels the cyclist passing by her house. Would like to warn him of the dangers.

She slumps in a cane chair, looking out into the trees.

She sees something at her window. The shadows re-organise. Whirling lines in front of her collide . . . She sits holding her legs. Outside the garden chair has fallen over under the black sky.

Her neighbour tells her to watch out for a cyclist who 'menaces the children.'

— Everytime I come to say 'Hello' he rides away!

— Is that why he's menacing?

— Yes, he's afraid because I know about him, being dangerous. I know.

— Have there been any attacks?

— God no! I wouldn't put up with that.

— So he just talks with the children.

— Menacingly.

Marlene walks around her garden, thinking 'More petty hysteria . . . '

She decides to see the man again. She waits in the shade at the top of the hill while her son tosses stones into the bush. White sulphur stones richochet. Her son stops, completely occupied.

She crouches beside him in the sand. They stare at feint swaying tracks in crumbling sand. He traces the lines with one finger and she follows with hers.

'This is the track of a snake.'

She draws a long lithe belly on the ground.

'Yes, we must be on the lookout.'

He sits firmly shaking his head and she holds him to her laughing, so relieved that he hadn't found a snake; just tracks.

She feels anxious at home.

In one corner of the bed the sheets feel like human hands and she sleeps fitfully —

Imagines bodies with every sound.

Sounds with every body image.

Sunday. No-one appears to be awake.

She walks outside to look for the newspaper and her son runs to the front gate. She sees the paper laying in the middle of the drive.

It's a burning day, her son running down the road. Marlene bends down, paralysed above bicycle lines. Drunken animal tracks.

She doesn't touch the paper.

HER STORY OF NIGHT

HER STORY OF NGHT

nursing my belly

There's a mirror in the hall and one in the bathroom. A mirror near the lounge. On the back door is a mirror ... Marlene sits on her bed holding her legs, running out under her arms. Fingers move over her hair to the base of her neck. She rubs herself softly, talking, bent forward listening too —

"Out in the street I felt sick in the stomach so I went into a Chemist's. It was late at night. He was an old man like my father ... As I stepped inside a tiny bell rang above my head and I looked up. He held his hands together and asked me a question. I looked at him and he looked like my father. He said, 'Do you want anything?'

I kept searching for things that I remembered most about my father that should have been on his face. It wouldn't take the shape I wanted ... He stood there, unsure of himself, and called out; 'Are you Marlene?' He moved behind the counter. 'You won't get a job wearing shorts.'

I told him I was sick, I motioned, a stomach ache.

'But you've come for the job as my assistant. You say you're sick? Have you come for the job or are you sick?'

His hands struck the table.

'I'm sick in the stomach, can you help me?' I said.

He glanced into the street then shut the door. He took me upstairs. Wood struts turning black. I took my hand out of my shorts and it hit a wall. Sucked my bruised hand ... He ushered me in to write out my qualifications and I wrote about my sickness —

He went off to sleep in an adjoining room.

My pen was shaking. The ink ran down my fingers leaving stains. I went into his room and sat with him on the bed. I touched his face but there was no sound. I lay down next to him holding his hand. He was trembling although it wasn't cold anymore. He said, 'Do you want the job? Have you a dress? . . . I'm 58 — '

I was sixteen —

He reached for my hand and touched my belly. I told him that I was sick, I needed medical attention. That I had a dress but didn't understand about the job.

'But we talked about it over the phone,' he said.

I remembered his voice soft like my fathers ...

He pushed hard with his hands and my mouth squealed open. Nursing my belly he told me I could have the job. He said that if he was younger he'd marry me.

He was a Chemist, he was not my father.

Later he showed me pictures of his family.

the moaning frame

I got a job with a friend of his, a wine merchant. I had to take him a painting of my own. I didn't understand what this had to do with wine. I packed a painting of a face I didn't recognise and proceeded to his home—

It was a windy night and the painting wanted to sail away. The streets clear like photographs exposed. My feet ahead of me, black on white. I felt the painting struggling to get away, shuffling under my arms, so I held it down with both hands. We both fell to the ground. It tore itself from underneath the paper. Bleeding, my mother's face.

I silenced the moaning frame with my overcoat.

Streets lurching like some ancient film projected. Hearing a whistle in the alley made me run both ways. I forgot the job, the chemist and the wine merchant. Left the painting bleeding on the street. My mother's portrait lays abandoned . . .

in the bathroom

My parents separated; I was 19. She was always drunk and calling my father A Philanderer. Broke up the family, she said. She vomited in the bathroom and my brothers left home for a while . . . She told me that he'd done something terrible to her. When I was alone with him I was frightened though I didn't know why.

My mother was drinking once and threw a glass at my father's face. I kept painting as it fractured on the floor.

There was some more men but I was unsure of myself. There was no magic and I wanted romance all the time. I became a photographic model. Love for me was a dream-exposure. My face was different then . . .

The painting too frustrating. Every time a new shape reared up, a more precise portrait. It would just go on and on. I'd have the beginning and the middle and the end all at once —

I fell in love with another painter. We lived at his mothers, that was crazy. I felt a criminal who had stolen his love.

the search for shape

I said bravado that I'd go home and he said, 'A good idea.'

I sat in my bedroom wanting him.

I found his photograph and cut around it, wavy lines, leaving only his face. Pinned him to the wall. Suddenly I realised that everything was changed, that everything was different, that he was never coming back. I found the scissors. I lay back from the waist, long hair hanging free. Looking at his eyes I smoothed the hair he so loved into one tress, handled it finely . . . With quick loops I cut it off near the ears, still smiling fully at him —

I looked at the floor to see blood-red

Now I had lost everything

My childhood gone, tom away from me —

I want a house where I have time to think . . .

I want to be a person but I don't want to be alone. I'd like to be a person who could for years exist without others, although I do need other things. I have a baby, that responsibility. I need an inner balance instead of an idealistic figure to live up to. Here there's nights without sleep, days of mechanical energy, increasing speed. I want to be wise . . .

the resulting exposure

I met this man. I was 25, sick from travelling and loneliness. I wanted something to take care of, so I met this man. At his doorway Vaughn saw what I wanted and asked me in. I did everything right — I looked him full in the face, touched him so often. Every moment like a snapshot / Remember his look as I sat down on the bed / Him undressing / I said it was hot and the window opened. Looking out into his courtyard at night. I was a cat and slinky . . . We moved faster in the dark — my memory here more jagged — his hands speeding over mine. Pinned to the bed, he cartwheeled from the wall. Our clothes leaving like threshing machines —

Making love sounds like some aerial dog-fight.

Making love-sounds like . . .

night & day

I dreamt I got up and found a baby in my bed.

Thinking I must have been pregnant without knowing it.

Discovered it was left there by mistake at some all night party but continued to look after it as if my own.

I see myself with the baby through two pale blue screens of glass, a warm light filtering through.

'your magazine husband'

Life's set now, I've got a place. Living with this older man. Blue's like my father really; gentle, same beard. He works 9 to 5. Papers and the tv. His grizzly wrinkles . . . hot and suffocating.

memory (blackout)

Sequence, April 1975.
Vaughn coming to see me in the main hallway.
About the baby. No lights, just cigarettes.
Dialogues exactly as said. As precise.
My face a glimmer of satisfaction and hope.
His chaotic, self-destructive; kissing mine.

withdrawal

An abortion in May. Blue's child. I said no, we don't want —
I withdraw from the slightest chance of hurt. My child gone and again chaos is the man. I, like night, all-engulfing. Withdrawing into the subterranean world of woman.

For the man 'History is intelligible chaos.'
His story is intelligible chaos / Her story — night.

round bodies open fear

When I was three our landlord wanted to paint my picture while my mother was away. I was wearing red pants. The man sat down stroking his whiskers, calculated, absorbing me. He asked his wife to get the pencils ... They were both in this together. They forced me underneath the table where he drew me sitting like a red cat. Like some ornament, then they both came forward again. I ran round and round the table until my mother walked in and I ran out the door.

'he could destroy you'

I dreamt. I was laying in bed head-to-toe with a man I'm not sure I know. Hearing something outside the door we wake up — It's a man. He asks me questions, trying to penetrate. He asks me, 'What do you do when you're beaten?' I rush him fiercely, but to him I'm just a playful kitten and he lifts me up.

The other man relaxes with a cigarette. I plead with him to call the Police. He shrugs his shoulders and says, 'Don't you remember? This man is a murderer who has cut the telephone cords.' I fight him by caressing with one hand and gnawing with the other. He tries to gore me, head butting my stomach. The man begins to topple —

With my mind alone I control him now ... I feel I have conquered this man, but unless I find someone who understands what I am saying, I shan't keep him conquered.

Taking out photographs of my past I find one with a simple key. A photograph in black and white. I'm aged three. Standing on a wharf I'm holding up two leaves exactly the same, from the same branch. I note my face, the puzzled joy. Alert sense of yin and yan . .. Looking closer at the picture I see that my arms are not outstretched but moving from the elbow inwards, slightly, for a coupling ...

AN EPISTOLARY SUICIDE

AN EPISTOLARY SUICIDE

Sam,

Why don't you come and see me in the mountains? It needs arrangements though and not at my place. During the week is the best time. I'm not denying you your capriciousness which I've been wounding each time we've met. It's still a real occasion even after so long. There you'd be, arriving at my door dressed in your thinness, your curves cavorting this way and that. You are such a delicious whore my dear —

I like your wantoness, despite the ravings, despite the pain that attacks me when I'm dreadfully alone. Is the pain my imagination, this offence to my sex? How do you feel when you're alone and I could be with someone else?

You'd accept it you'd say.

Sometimes I get really confident and let myself say things. I want to lay all the pain out on a table then crumple it up and throw it away. This letter's like that. This letter-cum-confession is a salve for my ever-stinging conscience. Remember when we used to talk about trust? How there was once established a safety between us? My emotions slide up and down the register, ending in NO SALE. When I can't make up my mind if I hate you or love you, what am I to do?

All this damn self-questioning. Why did you leave me in the place. It forced me up here. Well, you didn't force me up here with Blue, no — I thought of Luna Park today and felt a little eaten. You've eaten all the way around my wings. I get up and look at the baby and the blue sky and want to puke. It's all so sick and half-digested. We didn't really make anything like love because there was no continuing.

I'm not coming down yet. In a while I'll try it again. When you come up here there'll be a word barrage. Baby will shit on the floor. The goat will yawn all night. This is the country-life! You're afraid to come up here anyway —

The city's lively but dying round the borders. I'd like to leave the country but I've found cheap rent. Lennie wrote to me from Asia, it makes me want to go. Maybe all cities will be the same? I hate everything here at the moment. Why didn't you write to me weeks ago?

It's easier for you because you can forget while I feel locked to those earlier times. I'm waiting for something to happen. Is this just dreaming again?

& I'm sick of hanging around —

Marlene x

WINDOWS

WINDOWS

December

     Donna as waitress walking down aisles of dark-grained tables 'reserved' for businessmen. The Meat Cafe. Stares of hard-set youths, men watching her walk. Towards the cashier; a young Chinese who's pocketing all the tips . . . Money exchanged. All the waitresses are smiling, waiting their time. Someday, the Management will see.

     A cold afternoon. Kings Cross on the main street, chill from the sea-front. Through glass panes can be seen the life outside. People staring, stepping out of empty office blocks. Newspapermen selling the Sun as oldtime newsboys . . .

Or on the inside —

     Warm-orange lights, clinking glass dripping froth. Waitresses slink green long legs, wade thighs through milling customers. Newspapermen watch entranced all afternoon. Or. Fractured glint of shiny red-cheeked ladies over chrome bars waiting for a tip. Donna smiling. Smiling. Waiting, this time . . . Waitresses walk past young boys, possible accountants with accountant's secretaries. Smiles drift over a sea of tables — Their arms outstretched, 'To Us, to Us,' their faces radiant amongst the head-mass and arms waving.

Or. On the streets — News sold by sixty-year-old bachelors. News dying on the streets each day.

Inside. Warmth. Central heating. Electricity. Lights. Each wall warm-brown with red and blue Coats-of-Arms. In one comer, continuous bubbling cappucino coffee. Donna pouring, eager . . . hot. Flailing arms from blue suits, black jeans, all talking good lays and fast cars. Business, men.

Friday night

Donna wandering around empty tables 3 a.m. Finishing off a bottle of gin with the others, late tea courtesy of the French Chef. Chicken, French fries, sauce . . . He smiles moustachio from the ovens at the three girls florescent-green. He rubs his hands. One hairy, over the other, — the girls— the newspapermen watch the act with growing anticipation. The girls finish eating. They'll each buy the Sun —

'That makes thirty cents ... '

VIEW FROM THE SCENIC RAILWAY

VIEW FROM
THE SCENIC RAILWAY

I remembered them not so much as people, but as the way things happened.
Sam Fakir

Steps towards a Religious Conviction

Gory squats in the lounge-room, he lays face down. A prisoner in his own home forced between six end-rows of high-rise flats. Kings Cross. He says, 'I'm forced to live here, it's close to my work and I can't really afford anything else . . . ' He says, 'This is convenient,' and 'I hate it.'

Putting the bars across the windows, he draws the blinds. Checks the latch. Turns off the light and listens to soft music. He lays quite still, relaxed.

White light floods the room as Rada opens the front door. Touching her, his fingers get entangled in religious artifacts. He presses them to his mouth. She closes his eyes and the whirring stops —

'You're home . . . '

'Is baby awake?' she asks.

Gory confused — Does she mean him or the baby —

'I've really got to do my Italian Gory, so could you feed the baby . . . ' She laughs, pleading child-like till he gets up.

Laughing into his beard he says 'Of course, it's my turn, let me feed our baby . . . '

A Hearse in the Railway Yard

Hidden behind the back end of Luna Park behind the gaping mouth and Coney Island is the Railway Cleaning Yards where Department officialdom demands manual expertise / sitting dormant for sometimes a week three trains at best steam-cleaned by hand Gory kicks a silver bin over the greasy floor and trips down the aisle flipping one green leather seat prepared to snooze / tapping the brass rail with his feet he sits up lonely head framed low against the tiny windows of the train.

Eyes fixed upon the blackened rows of seats set back to back he makes out in deep glass the lines of his own contorted face / hands on ears and eyes shut urging music into head he gets instead the laugh of Luna Park.

The Mechanical Terraces

They moved into a terrace well-prepared to live the hippy life:
'Vegetarian food!' she says.
'Of course,' he says, dreaming a T-bone veal rump dream.
'University?' she says.
'You go . . . ' he says, remembering his martyrdom at school.
'I'll work nights,' she says, 'Perhaps a Motel!'
'Cleaning dirty laundrey in a motel? . . . Okay.'
Gory the wheezing worker slaves to bring home bread to wife intelligent and child. Dragging damaged bronchial tubes about the streets at night, he says, 'This is convenient.'
They spend every Sunday patrolling the area, pushing their stroller past suburban foodoramas. Keeping baby satisfied with mad rushes down the alleys seeking Panadol. Passing drunks and cripples they both felt 'Yes', this was indeed the place for Youth.

In their house sometimes the lights went out altogether and

Gory would stumble around to the fuse box cursing to stave off the fear. Rada walks around the hall uneasily, waiting for the lights . . .

Gory takes care of baby while Rada works in Motel. At home it gives them talking points, each rise and rate of progress equated with their own fine parental qualities.

After work, they make love, efficiently . . . till Rada wakes up screaming, pushing Gory away. Saving herself. Huddled in one corner she fends off the imagined animal that mauled her, clutching at his stunted fingers, scratching flesh. Crossing her legs over injured weeping thighs — Gory tries to calm her down, shaking his head crying-lungs. 'You're only dreaming Rada, dreaming . . .'

Later huddling with him, sad not understanding how she could have said these things or even thought of rape. So she would coax him, caress him, into making love.

All Aboard

Motel is a Scenic Railway. From high up amongst its thirty floors one can see the changing faces of the city. One huge electric light above a crowded warehouse, Motel draws its net / perimeters inhabitants.

Rada works at Motel every night, catering for special clientelle or simply cleaning — / / — 'So Miss your gonna clean my room today well let me first get dressed!' Jerk bounds out of bed stark naked and Rada changes the sheets. He stands by the window trying to put on his trousers. She stops her work, smoothing the pillow against her chest, staring at the slight depression on the bed. He turns to her, his trousers falling to the floor. She looks at his waist and muscular belly as he grips her arms. Dropping the pillow she falls with him on the bed, keeping her knuckles taut against his back while he tears at her clothing / /

Gory stands under the lights of Motel watching the darkness thin into morning. Knowing she is up there he tries to distinguish her from the other shadows in the air. He thinks of her wandering alone as he does, leading a solitary life ...

Gory a dwarf of MOTEL / humming like a power-plant on heat / sweet sex-sounds heaving from its portholes / holds him there, in tow.

In momentum, through Tunnels of Love

Jerk at his desk above the printing room, typing. The turbines revolving below make him uneasy, the printing press surges through the building. His legs buckle —

He writes about the Irony of Married Life — 'Pounding out furious thumbprints on Ali's back, Kerry hung on grimly. He hadn't even taken off his shoes . . . '—Words lost in the hum of the press as reams of paper strapped with wire funnel into waiting sacks. Swivelling round, Jerk sees Motel rising out of the streets. He takes his wedding ring off his finger and puts it in a drawer. Nodding to the window he snaps the desk drawer shut. He leaves the building and walks the straight line back to Motel.

On the Ovarian Trolley

Donna sits at her piano, just between chords. From her apartment, neon lights slowly grouping . . . Examining each page of music like famous fingerprints she settles into sound, playing to her own reflection.

The American comes to see her for tea.

He tells her he writes for TIME magazine and she believes him. He wants to write a 'great article' about her and her dedication. Music. She listens, smiling, as he goes about the process. She calls him 'An American Pornographer', and Jerk stops laughing.

'Donna, what's wrong with this! This is just for fun!'

'This — is fun?', she says, indicating his hand on her leg.

Jerk looks sincere, 'No Donna, this is deadly serious—'

He gets up again, pacing back and forth, telling her about how he can't believe in anything anymore. About his ruined marriage, sadness, pained sick-job with *Bawdy* and *Raucus Flesh*. How he needs a chance ... He becomes amorous, attentive, snuggling near her on the couch. He whispers huskily, 'Donna, lets ahh . . . '

She says she likes attention but that she doesn't want to screw him. Jerk is horrified, his face drops. Gathering his things together he scarcely says goodbye.

Upstairs, he stands behind his apartment door. He knows he'll get the maid, it's nearly time, he'll catch her when she comes in. Take Rada unexpectedly —

—Won't that be Fun-

Unbuckling

Gory keeps baby quiet till mummy comes home.

Rada comes in from work and runs straight up to her room. He drops baby on the couch and chases her. In the bathroom she is soaping down her thighs. They kiss . . . He brings her tea and she compliments him, stringing words together like an automaton. He gets caught in the machinery and holds his mouth tight, so she kisses him again. They kiss passionately, desperately. Upstairs, they undress —

In each others arms together in the dark she tells him about the past month, how she made love to an American in Motel, just the one time . . . Gory really sick at heart asks her why she didn't tell him this before.

She says, 'Before what?'

He trips into bed and sobbing sleep.

Baby lays awake on the couch.

Timetable

Rada comes home to find in horror drunken Gory rocking away in his chair, leering at her, whisky down his chin hysteria. Fingers stroking baby's neck —

There is a quick disintegration of the family.

Baby squeals for someone.

Gory drinking sage-like, comforts baby.

Rada fucks in Motel.

Jerk offers a solution — 'Rada have her own room. Better still, her own house. Better still she'll come and live with me. Yas. Gory, since he is the father takes the baby letting wifey see her sweetie maybe . . . huh . . . Money? No trouble! I'll take care of Rada.'

Gory says triumphantly that he's found a young unmarried mother and a terrace in Glebe. How he'll move in with her; they know he'll never do it. He stays home lonely with the kid.

The Shape of the City

Rada moves into Motel with a fine view of the city. She can see the streets they used to walk each Sunday. 'How Ironical,' says Jerk, labouring over his sex magazine. At the window overlooking she finds each street indelibly etched, screen-printed on her memory. She knows that their stroller is down there somewhere but she can't seem to see it. Rushing from one side of the pane to the other, but nothing changes. Still the same convoluted picture of compressed houses and dirty narrow streets. She wipes her arms squealing over the glass.

Peering into the fading light, eyes stumbling through the shadows of Motel, Rada is unaware that Jerk has left his table.

Standing behind her, naked — His hands go round to slice her belly She screams in her throat but won't let it out as her legs buckle. With her eyes in the streets she swallows - the shape of the city—

Slowly she is hauled to the floor of Motel.

IN THE
GAS OVEN

IN THE GAS OVEN

Just for Openers

Mill and Donna Tone have separated.

That is to say, they aren't One anymore, not man & wife.

Just Mill Tone, and Donna Tone.

Sam had met Donna near the laundry chute at Motel. He'd helped her move into a 'real home' with some old friends of Mill's from Sydney University. A Glebe terrace full of intellectual distinction. In a dead part of the city-elbow, gassed, already decomposing, it's inhabitants lay low in the yellow-green sunshine. Breathing with the aid of complex plastic tubing — strapped to their breasts and covering their genetilia; degrees and diplomas make them readily identifiable as residents of this terminal zone . . .

The Pelvic Call

Sam went inside. Donna wasn't home so he sits down with the others and dismantles the Roquefort cheese. Listens hard to the academics croaking heavily over Italian Lit. He mumbles, 'Pavese ... poor suicidal glyp,' and receives condescending gestures in return.

Stanley, an English-Noun Lecturer, elucidated sexual-panic:

'When I was 16 I had a sudden crush on a young girl. Catholic maiden whack who used to blow gum with me every day. She was strictly adolescent. I mean we all were then-ha-ha . . . but she was intelligent and had never had tremendous legs! We would exchange TIME magazine in her room at Wesley College. She was a genius! Ivy Wild, that's her name. She had such tremendous legs and I was short and unathletic. So that was important. I mean, she did like me . . . Well I listened to her gurgling REALLY WANTING TO CLUTCH HER — I can still see her now, those perfectly curved thighs by the rotting fruit. Compliments of T.S. Eliot! I almost wished I had kissed her then ...'

Musso smiled professionally in mild agreement. Bored. Voljack walks in and everyone is excited. Who cares about Stanley's rotting fruit? Voljack's been smoking hashish in the toilet and has V.D.

Stanley is a little angry, rolling a joint in one hand, patting his wife June with the other. Oxygen is passed around. June spills her breasts into Stanley's hands like dozens of boiled eggs. Stanley cackles, happier . . . Heavenly looks across at Sam as Musso whispers in her ear. She shows Sam her latest garter . . . 'She has Dietrich legs,' shouts Musso.

Queen to Bedroom Four

Mill and Musso make chess of the weather —
So it's been a good — Yes a good day.
Day how good say?   How do I say 'so good'?
So fine —   Then, fine and well and good.
Checkmate.

Smoothing her dress into a V, Heavenly accosts Sam — 'I'd kiss ya but I just washed my hair. You want to root me I can tell.'

'Ahhh, well . . . '

'Everybody else does.'

'Ahh-erh

'Then how about I cross your palm?'

'You mean, masturbate?'

No, I mean GIVE US YA HANDS CREEP, I'm gonna read them!'
She leads him to bedroom four, a drying room for heaps of
underwear and dozens of invisible legs. She puts one of his hands
underneath her dress and says, 'Not so fast Honey, just love me.'
Grabbing both his hands she reads them like open Pocket Oxford
Dictionaries, making twirling lines —

'I like you, place your hands on the table. Let me see ya
WHOLE palms! '

On her elbows swaying, turning one palm over the other
in a geriatric exercise, repeating crazy earnest contradictions —

These lines long. MMMMM. Your life will be deathly short.
Your reasons and your emotions conflict, making you a plumber
or a psychiatric nurse. I love both ... You found love at 20 and
at 30, unless of course you're under 25. Which is possible . . .
You're cold-hearted and love British Intellectuals. I'm one. You
have radiation burns, you smell of reeking rubbish. No! I smell of
reeking rubbish!'

She thrust her hands at Sam, 'Can you love me?!'

'At the moment, no ... '

Her arms pleading pull him in. They topple over and
she disengages.

'You know me so you love me. I want you so you must want
me. I kiss you only — You can't have my virginity, my hymen's
in the Nicholson Museum. I'd like to root you but I'm only kidding.
Say you love me and I'll go away . . . Musso my only Man because
I'm just a Student of Love. I'm only innarested in ya mind! I know
everything about life because I've had a monster. I don't know where
it is, but if you say you love me I'll go away and find it—'

Sam falls onto the table, 'I feel sick,' he says.

Voljack bursts open the door.

'Is this a gang-bang, I'm busting,' he roars.

Sam fights his way to his feet, Heavenly shrieking. Voljack

her which calms her down. Her tears dry, plastic coagulates. Sam falls into heaps of underwear — 'It's all this gas . . .

Middle Games at Muscle Cove

Downstairs, the three men display stiff-jeaned genitals. All discuss their relative degrees and Voljack's medical intentions. The women make tea while they sit on the couch. Donna walks in and yells out, 'Muscle Cove!' Heavenly and June pour the tea, looking adoringly towards Muscle Cove. Voljack is in the middle of a hideous confession —

'I was with the boys copping a look at a sheila in the Toxteth Pub when a country cop turned his Lark on us and we were forced to leave. I grabs the girl, my mates shouting Root Her For Me Kid! Well it's a miracle I'm still here with the cop homing in on the screen ... I got the sheila into a Zephyr '65— You all know the Zephyr '65? It's a nice car, good upholstery ... I got her tubing off just as her sister hits the street. Screaming like a maniac, 'Where's Ivy? Where my little sister?'

'Well, panic, yes I was. Dog! There I was groping the pull in the front seat with a hair lip, groin in Plastic Paradise. I had to let her know! So I strapped her legs to the steering wheel, took my foot off the brake and let it go . . . SHE'S IN THE CAR! I yelled. SHE'S IN THE CAR! ... I never saw the car again.'

The room screams hysterically.

'You lost a '65 Zephyr for a girl?' asks Donna, 'You are crazy —' 'I got a disease,' he laughs.

'Can't have been my little Ivy that gave you a disease,' says Stanley. June stares at him incredulous.

'You wouldn't have gotten into her to know, Stanley,' says Volj. 'I would've; I'm not scared of sheilas.'

'You are.'

'I'm not, I'm married!' June nods agreement.

'Mate, I know' says Volj / 'Who told you?'

'Vaughn — ' / Vaughn ...

' VAUGHN TOLD YA! HE'S A MANIAC! I WOULDN'T
BELIEVE ANYTHING VAUGHN TOLD YA!'

'He told me everything about you and Ivy Wild . . . Sad ... '

'HE'S A BLOODY MADMAN, A CRIMINAL -'

'You're scared —'

'He's got a gun —'

'So you're scared of Vaughn because he's got a gun?'

'No.'

'But you said Stanley — '

'He's — malevolent. He's got a gun. He wouldn't know anything about Ivy Wild.'

'Stanley, I think you need a gun to get a root!'

'You'll make a bloody awful surgeon,' Stanley says.

'I was in a mental Institution once,' Musso says, 'Hardon Hall.

Madness from the inside and I can tell you they're not just a bunch
of freaks. They're all intelligent. It's competative in there, a
pressurised atmosphere, everyone groping about . . . Real encounters
are impossible and there's no rooting — You can never really take off
your mask in there. The most perverted are the most reverred. I've seen
them holding on to limp cocks for hours, looking for results.
Perversions building up by degrees. . '

Sam asks, 'What do you do to keep out of it?'

'My own personal study of madness — Yoga, Meta & Pata-
physics— Snake-charming — keeps me occupied,' says Musso, rapping
his knuckles on the table top.

'Put on some rock and roll,' yells Stanley to June, 'Let's thrust
hips!' June looks at him uncomprehending.

'Dance!' Stanley shreiks.

EVERYBODY IN THE OLD CELL BLOCK
GOTTA DANCE TO THE JAILHOUSE ROCK!

Purgatorio

Refa comes downstairs to see Mill. Refa is on smack. Shivering in her cotton dress she is glad that Donna is leaving. She needs Mill, a regular fix.

'Mill I had this dream that I was going crazy. I did. This beard came into our bed while you were asleep. I was putting away the kit. I'd burnt my hand, was sucking it. It was looking at me. It said, 'Can I come in, I'm cold.' My arm was stiff and my hand had gone white. I crept under the sheets so that I could be buried with you —'

She falls into his arms, shaking violently.

Mill says, 'It happened this morning. It wasn't a dream it was Gory. Rada's left him and he wants attention. I kicked him outside but he's coming over to the party tonight.'

Heavenly knocks over the chess game with her legs. Musso shoves her away. 'This is a serious game!' he says. Mill counters with a Bishop. Heavenly topples the board and Musso leaps upon her. They wrestle on the floor. Stanley watches the fight —

It isn't really a fight but Stanley makes it into one.

He takes off his glasses and looks down at the crease in his pants.

He smooths out his pants with sweaty hands.

The lump in his pants equals the lump in his throat.

He falls onto them both, hard jeans meet jeans. Musso laughs and grunts while Heavenly wheezes under three sets of plastic apparatus.

June sits breathing smoke rings, dreaming of talking to Musso, who always treated her like an idiot. She wanted to tell him about how Stanley lately doesn't want to root. Stanley tells her to shut up, trying to work. He studies Primal-Language so that he could talk to Musso ... June thought of trading in her mouth at some Government Department or going back to University. Perhaps a degree in Chem. Psych ... In a Department she could talk to Musso, as one member to another —

Heavenly looks up at June and whistles through her teeth. She wants that little extra something. June has. She wants to crush men with her tits ... She smiles back at June with a twisted mouth.

The Monstrosity Exhibition

At the party Voljack begins to rustle up The Orgy. He's brought a huge woman who displays diplomas from Oxford and Pentridge, one from the USA. Undressing her, wanting to 'Throw her into the ring', they sit together near the fire eating nutmeg, digested with a little Dostoievski —

Stanley cuddles Heavenly's little monster. Shifting slightly in his seat. Sam watches from behind a bookcase, waiting for Donna —

Gory, Rada and Jerk arrive, all discussing Foetal Shapes. Gory sinks his teeth into Heavenly, who squeals delight. Gory whispers, 'Relate!' She amorously strokes his nose. Her monster asks Gory where his baby was and he quaintly smacks its ear, then puts a bag over its head. 'I left it in the cupboard,' says Gory.

Everyone now is really laughing.

Jerk kisses Rada, stroking her electrolysed thighs. She's come to show Intelligent Jerk off to her lecturers. Between swallows, Jerk talks of American Jazz, Hubert Selby Jnr and himself, the doyen of Bop. With his mechanical sexaphone, Jerk reads all his editorials in a loud voice. Resting her mouth in low-cal water, Rada takes off her shoes to free those feet —

Refa falls downstairs, Mill holding placidly her needle and dropper. A burning smell of used bandages as she rubs her arms.

Some begin pawing Voljack's friend, rolling her over and over, copping the Feel. Mill joins in shaking a small crucifix. Voljack pounds his cock over her hot heap of flesh. She keeps smiling. 'Is This Really It?'

Rada and Jerk fondle on the stairs. 'Let me in too, I'm cold,' Gory says. He forces a hairless leg between them, crushed against the wood. Stanley jostles drunken Musso, kissing him on the nose —

'Put on some Rock and Roll!' he yells.

Musso clouts him with Chuck Berry's 'Golden Decade'.

Heavenly watches in horror as June removes her shirt from those Lovely Breasts. She takes off her singlet too. Blushing, with Musso, pumping heartbeats. June dances, Musso hotly after her. Stanley tries to gain attention by reading Mussolini, tearing out the pages. The girl yells strapped to the fireguard, 'IS THIS IT? IS THIS REALLY IT?'

Everyone dances, semi-naked; semi-detached. All hoping that Voljack will attack someone — anyone — to start The Orgy . . .

Donna walks in —

June covers her breasts. Heavenly faints.

Donna walks out again.

'Portrait of a Lady,' says Musso.

Sam rolls up off the floor.

Stanley is whimpering ...

End Games

Mill walks into Donna's room and shuts the door. She is playing the piano. He says, 'Well isn't it nice to see me?'

She plays, but with mistakes.

'Donna, I want you to forget everything. I want to try again.'

She drowns his attention in crashing walls of sound.

Mill says, 'Something going on between us,' like a pair of rusty old loins. He begins to undress. 'That alright with you?'

She turns around, 'What do you mean anyway?'

Mill blinks; 'I want to live here, with you, now.'

She begins to pack her clothes. 'That's alright Mill you can have my room. It's got lotsa gas. Better that hot-shot's upstairs, it's the classiest hole in the block. I'll pick up the rest of my things later . . .'

Mill sits on the double-bed holding his belt, rubbing its hard leather surface. Holding the punched end he flays the grand piano. Sickening bruised wood sounds . . .

Gory Hits Hardon Hall

Sam heard that Gory had committed himself for a stint at Hardon Hall. He'd tried to strangle little monsters, so Musso suggested it ... Rada is radiant, 'Free at last.'

Jerk thought the whole thing, 'Ironical ... '

Gory then signed himself out after only ten hours in The Institution Of His Choice! Musso said he'd never get such a chance —

Plastic Paradise

On the third day Sam arrived to help Donna move out. Stanley sits in a chair bandaging a lacerated hand. 'Dog bit you?' Sam enquired. Stanley growls as Sam walked upstairs —

Heavenly drags him into bedroom four. 'Musso is bedridden,' she wails, 'Does this mean he's impotent?' She drops her blue negligee and pushes him into faded plastic —

'Musso's trying hambone next door, so sick in head I can't watch. Sick, but cool man and gas. He's with the monster. Mouthing now, he's flexing apparatus — '

Sam ran downstairs, bolting the door.

Stanley turns out the lights as Sam gropes for the phone —

'Operator, Operator . . . The Gas Company please, we have a leaky main. I'd suggest complete evacuation. Toxteth Street Glebe ... There's panic on the crumbling edifice.'

Donna appears waving suitcases and Sam drops the talking phone.

'What about the piano?'

'Fuck the piano!'

Stamping down the hallway they hear bodies undergoing chemical weathering. Gassed, their limbs cry out for strangulation. The house foundations give way as the apparatus tears. Stanley babbles an inventory of his wife's organs. Needle by the front door, Refa naked. Mill and Voljack gangbang the grand piano. Inside June locks the door eating Violent Crumble Bar . . .

They climb up the hill in silence, no sound save a few sparrows by a leaking gas-tap hissing in the sun. Standing with Donna's luggage on the corner, they hail a taxi and they don't look back.

THE JUNK EQUATION

THE JUNK EQUATION

The Circuit

Cement warps in the sun. Six lane highway crossing city traffic. Kings Cross. Motel rising from the streets . . . Sam and Vaughn find old friends in the Meat Cafe —

'Mad Mike! When did you get out?'

'Call this out?' Mike spills his coffee cup.

'Have you a place to stay?'

'With Voljack in the Cross — '

'I'm sick, need doctor real bad,' mumbles the Kid. 'Got the flu, delayed reactions. Two pints of ether with aspirin is no use anymore.'

Swallowing mandrax ...

'I'm unhappy,' wails the Kid, 'Lonely, who are you?' Mike sits Voljack straight-jacket upright in the comer.

'How did you get out Mike?' asks Sam.

Mike holds the Kid up by one arm —

'First I thought, Life's a Gas, it was the first time I'd had security! The pen a much more delicate operation however, appeasing the power complex. After a while it was not so hot. Just lonely on the inside ... I parolled.'

The Kid laughs then slumps over the table. Mike urges blood into his system — 'Come on Volj, don't go under.' Whispering to the Kid white-faced, hair stiff-cardboard Valentino.

The Architexture of the Riot

'Remember newspaper images of the Bathurst Riot? — 'Prisoners like Wild Animals' screamed the *Sydney Morning Herald*, beating to death Her Majesty's. Headlines — TWO MILLION DOLLARS DAMAGE. BATHURST GAOL DESTROYED. Warders wound nine rioters, debutantes. It was their first night out, can you blame them?'

'Frankly, no ... ' says the Kid.

'250 inmates suffering from an overdose of Maximum Security.'

'What's nine wounded considering the damage,' says Vaughn.

'They do consider the damage. They owe the Government over $200,000 each.'

'Hit me with it —' says the Kid.

'Okay — Joe made a petrol bomb. With the debutantes in the chapel watching 'Women in Love'. White flickerings. Around us much groaning . . . Suddenly Joe starts yelling things and chairs are uplifted in the dark, people gag and a gun goes off. I run down the vault with Joe burning walls. Joe cackling, 'I've got a knife, I can kill.' We defaced. Joe upends his mattress, tearing it to shreds; we smashed a toilet in, we smashed a face in yelling WARDER!

'Fires had started and Joe says 'Let's burn up with it.' Tempting . . . Armed prisoners obstructed firemen — IT'S OUR FIRE! they yelled. Trusties talked openly with reporters and fed the warders roast pig. You saw the papers? The destruction of the cookhouse, what a blow-job! It's iron-roof had buckled under fire. Pressure had ignited the body of the building. Bars flat out with charred embers, corrugated iron. Twisted steel rods melting — the architecture of our nightmare — Endless dream-curves, black spirals winding through the vaults . . . On the ground lay a lonely pigs head, but alas, no apple.'

'I can't eat anything,' says the Kid

Rock & Role Hoodlum

Mike sings along with the jukebox — 'UH O HO YES, I'M THE GREAT, PRETENDER ...' At the counter, waitress-pandemonium.

'You know in the pen we were really bored. Bored of Directors! Thank Dog when radios were installed . . . ADRIFT IN A WORLD OF MY OWN, A HUH AHAAAA . . . I dreamt of singing to the whole house. Mad Mike, in spotlight! But I couldn't sing, I had to play guitar — '

'Oh that's, sad,' says the Kid.

'I became Mad, for everyone, the village idiot. I made up great songs. I could sing anything. Like 'Safe Breaker Blues,' which always went down well — I GOT THEM SAFE BREAKER BLUES BECAUSE NO JEMMIES IN MY RIGHT HAND..'

Vaughn carves his initials in the table.

'Then I wrote some hap-hap-happy blues. Real Poetry! I called it the Kangaroo Blues.'

The Kid sang along too —

'NOTHING'S MEAN, I AIN'T DOWN. I'M SO HAPPY, MEANING CLOWN.

I'VE GOT THE HAP-HAP-HAPPY, CLEAN FUN KANGAROO BLUES . . .'

The waitress calls the Police as Sam pays the bill —

'That song never goes down well,' says Mike, 'I don't understand it.'

'It's because no-one's happy,' says Vaughn.

'Everyone's blue,' says the Kid.

On the Border

Voijack collapses in the street, junk-sick. 'To the Park,' he croaks, 'Hit me with it!' till they reach the El Alemain Fountain.

'I just had to see it. Took my first hit here. I got all the luck.'

He sits on the concrete rim surveying the crowds —

'These freaks! No wonder I can't identify with humans anymore. They make me worry, they really do. Life for me emblazoned in city alleys and cars, music, places seen. Identity-zones like staring into a fountain.'

'Crap on your Uni education,' says Mike.

'Ha-ha,' says the Kid, jerking fast into the fountain.

Suicide

Mad, why is suicide so fashionable?'

Mike revives the Kid by artificial resuscitation.

'These sire the days of self-exposure, of exorcising madness. This exposure hardens the body, building a crusty exterior.'

'So we have to open up, ahh, the body,' wheezes the Kid.

Mike nods. 'The Kid's doing a medical degree to cope with his disease. He feels he needs it.'

'The disease or the degree?' Sam asks.

'So whatever life you follow has a junk equation,' says Vaughn.

'That's why suicide is so fashionable. It's a way out — '

'I'm a Rock and Roll Suicide,' Vaughn sings, laughing.

Terminal Zone

Voljack is wet and anguished and people peer. He retreats behind dark glasses. 'Everybody's looking at me!' he says. 'I stayed in Wollongong with Vaughn once and everybody there looked so weird. The place with streets creeping history nostalgias. Remember Smith Street? Home of abstract artists and life addicts? It's a miracle they didn't all shoot their parents like famous Vaughn and his Gun . . . '

Vaughn fires a thumb at Sam's head.

'On Crown Street the fifteen year old crutches dying, their legs on fire. Faces bending in the slight wind, their parents gloom shattering midnight life-extravaganzas. There I was, passing by the corpse of all our parents hysteria. Bodies jump in bundles across the tarmac, hobbling aircraft attempting to fly. Crashing demonstrations on the nerve edge ... '

The Kid wanders about the footpath, one foot in the gutter —

'Now after that I worry about them all. What are they trying to do to me and my friends. Put them in jail. Put them out of work. Send them to the asylum, university. No-one seems the same anymore. What's going on?'

He bites his fingernails.

'We hit Wonderland, the old Bowl. A sign of our times,' says Vaughn. 'They were good times, five years ago. The Bamboo Room uncrowded. Each step evoked the juke-box, some rock-memory — I'M GONNA BE A WHEEL SOMEDAY — Heads singing for release amongst retreating sidewalks . . . '

'Maybe the City is only in our heads,' says the Kid, 'Maybe we should never have tried so hard to make things happen, maybe the city's crumbling now.'

'You lot making with the 'mysteries'!' says Mike. 'Shut-up.'

He keeps them all moving through the crowd. They push the line back to the Kid's flat.

Headlines

A flat overlooking the city, lights on, the radio blaring the weather — 'The Weather will continue bad,' it reports, 'There will be more calamities, more death and despair ... '

Mike switched on to 2JJ. Marc Bolan's 'I'm a Groover'. Vaughn gyrating around the room, beer dripping on the floor.

'Death and despair! My Dog! Whenever Famous People die they stand back in deep religious awe, erecting monuments. I want to hear about Life! Why if the Kid died today there'd be headlines —SEX FIX FINALLY FUSES —'

The Kid laughs so hard he falls under the table.

'What if you die?' he gasps.

Mike paces about the room . . .

'MADMAN'S DYNAMITE DEATH!' he roars.

Coca Cola image

Leaving the flat, Sam and Don run down to the concrete flyover towards William Street, passing drunks on wooden seats. Mad Mike and the Kid wave to them from the window. Sam sees legs hanging from a car door. In rising street-hysteria they're nearly caught thrashing in the gutter by a Council Cleaning Unit. Rumbling vision of doom-brushes washing freeways ...

Below Motel, a clear perspective of the city-centre. One long entrail — Hot neon signs of COCA COLA and ABC (infinity) radio 'mysteries' of the street — Fused eyes through green lights. Vibrating streams of cars, red tail-lamps. THE BOULEVARD ...

Mad Mike waving / the Kid transfixed on the bed
Flat white neon projected from Motel / 'It's the real thing'
Mike slowly moves from the frame / bodies moving surge together
Through the window the sky is buffeted by vast COCA COLA
image

The storm begins

SCAR CITY

SCAR CITY

The inner city bares at night —

Old-timers drink at the Tradesman's Arms. Someone asleep
by the phone . . . Wet streets follow Council Cleaning Units hissing
gutters. Two o'clock, Sam & Donna listening on the floor. Cocks crow
in Palmer Street, businessmen run home to their wives —

Crushed glass / Spinning metal-hits bent post / Shagged
bitumen. Sam throws himself to the window. Shaking autos over gutter
hot oil spilling, one driver gets out . . . Donna in pyjamas runs
downstairs, Sam calling to her, 'The keys!' —

Tenants watch the drama from above. Italians wandering the
theatre lurch through spotlights. Under a grimy blanket a woman on the
ground. Kneeling husband twisting her neck. Heart stops then into
breathing. People stare at the grimy blanket, spindly legs, her soft shoes.

Red car caved-in. Crushed GIVE WAY post, a vacant
allotment opposite the Tradesman's Arms. Injured Mazda leaves the
accident, clash-gears down one-way street. A Maori leaps from the public
phone to view lights on the husband sweating over wife, —

Tow trucks unannounced slip vultures, silent tyres over wet
road luminosity. Three arrive from different directions, park bubbling
by the victims to study the cars. Friends of the husband flash torches
into one-way street seeking the Mazda. Police arrive, two incredulous, —

— Bodies breathing on the bare night-lit stage — Up on balconies families lay huddled — Police Ambulance Injured, Ford cars.

*

Sam holding Donna as it begins to rain. Squatters slowly clapping from terrace rooves a block away. Tow trucks redistribute the wreckage — One lane of smashed glass, crushed metal; becomes the instruments of an operating table

The green Falcon owner slapping his thighs, argues with the tow-er. Inside the truck, his wife knitting. Sam & Donna run home in the rain, passing a man in a fur hat, —

Both watch from their terrace remnants of the accident, rain blown in through open windows. City hums with the radio on. 2JJ... Policemen kick a crushed tomato box. Her husband turns off the car lights. Under street lamps, occasional cars — Ambulance-men care for the spindly legs. Noises echo, sound delayed. Green Falcon explanations to rigid police under the Tradesman's Arms. Orange flash lights landscape /// Policeman drops torch beams at the rocking terraces // Groaning fat men served smashed cars / Red Cortina pushed into the vacant block.

*

— Below broken terraces, glass & chrome metal strips — Winches squealing bodies up — unearthly hound-noise

— Under blaring neon EATON CAR RADIO an ambulance pulls away

On the terraces, crowded balconies, lace trailing in the wet night, — Their faces out abandoned windows ... Looking up to half-built office towers, chrome & glass-lit pock face of a demolition zone; the inner city bares —

A scar-city of love — In blaring neon, CHRISTIAN REAL ESTATE.

AT THE RAFFLES HOTEL

AT THE RAFFLES HOTEL

Bicycles move slowly across the bridge towards the Raffles Hotel. Rickshaws, their drivers wearing broad-brimmed coolie-hats, press on under the tropical heat. Legs pumping long cable veins, glint from the river sheen. The road weary under bicycles infinite. From a window opposite the Raffles, Sam counting them in.

Only three days here and Donna feels homesick; Over the city, their cheap Chinese hotel. Olive-skin scuffs across red-paved floors, his singlet tropical white. Donna sick from too much spicy food. Her hips jut from the bed-plateau as he throws a sheet over the bamboo bed.

'Hardly the Raffles,' she says, gripping the sheet.

'This is marvellous, bloody marvellous.'

The room Chinese red and green. Across the floor cheap rugs, heavy mirrors reflecting a clothes-stand, table, and ornate wardrobe. Sam crouches in the sun with the *Straits Times* …

'You know what sickens me most?' she says.

Sam doesn't look up.

'It's the stares,' she says.

Sam nods reassuringly till he reaches the window overlooking the street. Scans the city-scape. European tourists run through brown crowds, their faces pink under furious sunlight. Dark glasses smouldering …

Sam at the window watching bicycles going over the long arched bridge towards the Raffles. Metal parts shining in the sun. Pedestrians leap from traffic islands for the safety of shaded walkways. Black taxis drive past at fifty miles per hour. No zebra crossings . . .

Donna at the window watching bicycles round the corner of the Raffles Hotel —

'Why didn't we stay there Sam?'

'Just imagine it. This is cheaper.'

'Who cares about the money!'

Sam throws her his wallet. She laughs, folding her arms against the window frame, dreaming of white-steamed bathroomtiles ... Sam at the table planning ahead.

'Who was Raffles anyway?'

Sam consults THE GOLDEN GUIDE. 'Sir Stamford Raffles made Singapore into an industrial port from a tiny fishing village. 1819. 'The Lion City', also was an island naval base ... This history didn't save it from the Japanese.'

'What did the Japanese want with this lousy
climate?' Strategy, thinks Sam.

'Bicycles,' he says.

*

Watching the cyclists on the bridge by the Raffles Hotel. The main business activity on the river bank, a bright chrome and glass complex run by strict Council regulations. Tourists and office workers pumped through the compound, brown bodies delineating chromium counters. On the river, sampans lifeless drifting with the tide. The Singapore of empty sampans, after the Japanese and American invasions.

'I worked for ten years behind a counter Sam. I've got no education.'

'What use education?'

*

Both at the window in reflections of themselves. On the pavement below, cyclists position to fly over the bridge.

'Your brother was a cyclist Donna, wasn't he in racing?'

'Yes. There are so many cyclists down there.'

'Do you remember his last race, the end?'

'My brother was winning and had passed two riders, fast, well ahead of them towards the finish line — '

'He won his last race.'

'Walking his bicycle beneath him along the gutter, his feet on the bitumen, the curb directing him. I saw him take off his helmet. Under one arm, mopping his brow with some white material — '

'You saw his face?'

'It was covered by the white material. He wasn't moving ... Then the two beaten riders sped together cross the finish-line, towards him in the gutter. One collided with my brother. Buckled wheels — The impact hurtled him face-forward into the curb, his body buckled under the twisted bike.'

'You saw his face?'

'It was covered by the white material. People all around him salvaged the frame first. People staring at the body. People were saying *dead*, my double . . . '

'You were five.'

'Yes, twenty years ago.'

*

In the bright afternoon sun the shadows become longer, reflections dissolving under the bridge, buildings in the sun.

*

Sam views the dormant sampans. The river crossing. Remembers newsreels of the harbour wreckage bombed by the Japanese — Flickering movie frames lone coolie cycling over the bridge. Long distance shot. In the havoc, upturned sampans, hats floating. Smoke billowing from crushed buildings . . . Still standing was the perfect polished facade of the Raffles Hotel.

Sam overlooking Singapore at night. Harbour rings of kerosene lamps curving seascape. Neon blinking buildings by the winding river. A blunt dead-end of vacant sampans. The banks rich with monumental structures of chrome and glass. Distraught pedestrians ran through a hail of taxis under yellow light.

*

'Sam, where do we go next?' / 'The next hotel.'
'When do we go?' / 'We have a week's visa.'
'A race against time . . . ' / 'We'll leave the country —'
'Thank God — ' / 'By bicycle ... '

*

Bicycles move slowly across the bridge towards the Raffles Hotel. Rickshaws, their drivers wearing broad-brimmed coolie-hats, press on under the tropical heat. Legs pumping long cable veins, braking, glint from the river sheen. The road weary under bicycles infinite. Sam counting them in . . .

The bedroom silent, a doctor treating Donna on an unmade bed. A white pillow is cocked under her head. She faces the open louvered windows.

Turning over, her neck rolling with the pillow.

Sam watches a lone bicycle struggling over the bridge ... The Raffles Hotel determining his progress ... workers have left the city that is now not so frantic. There are less cars, less black and yellow taxis. No zebra crossings —The afternoon turning, into darkness. Over, the cyclist crashes into the gutter by the Raffles Hotel. The doorman silent. Pedestrians step around him, staring; in their way mending the body.

Sam leaves the room to go outside —

The window frames pedestrians huddling around the broken coolie. The doorman silent. Twisted cycle spinning. Sam running between traffic towards the Raffles, stops to pick up the coolie's broken hat.

LAYBACK LENNIE

LAYBACK LENNIE

This is my last letter home. The last time I write. Writing from an island furthest out, I have no paper left but this. The rest is panic. People here are tense and fear-exited. There are no planes out. All our dimensions limited, only long ways home. Frozen in the restaurant like some long lost school reunion we suffer each others tales-of-woe with empty laughter, clasped hands and heavy breathing, hysteria dying now — We sit serious, waiting for Good News.

Tony.

Tony DaShelf is sleeping. Sam waits for his eyelids to open and let him in. He pulls the blinds. Tony was to leave last Sunday via Lennie's ticketting. His mother waiting his return. Now it's Thursday, she's still weeping at Sydney airport.

— Garuda is refuelling —

'I can't see them doing that! What with Timor Intervention there's just no way through. Kupang's closed. Cathay Pacific Airlines have only one man sick in their office. He needs a doctor! Burning his wrists are discouraged travellers on the Pay'-Away-Plan ...

*

Tickets or Death

Tony DaShelf wakes up at four, walking around the room sideways as he is apt to walk. Sam follows with his milk. Tony's eyes are red and white with no pupils, still left laying on the bed. He swallows the milk. The Shelf stands at the door running fingers greasy through thin hair — 'It's been four days now, my heads in the toilet. What's life but a bowl of cherries ... '

'Tony, I hear you're off tomorrow. Got the flight out — '

'All lies I tell you. Layback Lennie had my ticket but its missing. He's missing! He's got my student card for sale now at some class Motel. Denpassar. He's selling cheap flights! Reselling my ticket — '

'So your flight's cancelled, over?'

'Looks that way Sam. Lennie rang to say he lost my motorbike, the tickets inside a bottle in the gas-tank — For safety's sake. Here is the key, the only survivor.'

'So the body's lost — Tony, think about it this way — You haven't lost the tickets yet, you've lost the motor-bike.'

'A brand new Flash. You think Lennie's hanging out on me?'

'You mean, it's all a figment?'

'Maybe Lennie sold the tickets and got a better price. He said he grounded Flash on Kuta Beach, kicked it, spluttering. Left it for dead. He gave it to a kid. Laughing, the kid said thanks. When Lennie returned with a mechanic there were many grateful faces but no bike —'

'No kid! Lennie may have made a mistake . . . '

'Mistake! We may have to eradicate Layback Lennie ... '

Meet the Landlord

Lennie sits in his motel room making false flight coupons to sell to distressed travellers. He is surrounded by local artists all offering suggestions, slapping their thighs. He's made a deal, a good deal — He sold the Shelf's ticket to an Indonesian four-star general, the owner of the grand motel. He's had luck. In his office below, the General gives agun and religious instruction to the manager. Lennie is to be dealt with, a customary blow. Smiling round the contours of the grand motel, here Lennie may have gone wrong ...

Timor Intervention

'Dili has fallen!'

'How much to fly to New Guinea?'

'Haven't you heard — The Indonesians will annex that next!' —

Five Australian journalists shot dead. Unarmed, in bamboo. October 16th. Soldiers mobilized on trains east carrying submachine guns, cradling a smile. Harrassing students, travellers. Even the toilets are filled —

Lennie has reappeared.

'Bali—Sydney, $407 U.S. Life's cheaper by Merpati . . . What's up with Cathay? Where's my man, the doctor ... Calling Doctor Benway ... '

The Shelf still unwell —

'Tony, don't worry. You'll laugh when this is all over.'

His head in a glass of milk, revitalising —

'I don't know Sam, I don't know what I'm doing ... Stealing jeans off other people's clotheslines is not the answer. Drink, is not the answer. I'm sick and tired. It's raining out there! Nor a cock-fight, I've seen fill the sights. I don't understand the crumby language. Broken rickshaws, bejaks, overloaded. Stumbling pink, us Europeans. I don't know what I'm doing. I need a doctor. I need money for a doctor. All Lennie offers is a holy gas-tank with dreams inside. I'm cracking maybe, you think? . . .I'll get a bus to Java and see miles of rice. Cross-country like the old days. This Timor Intervention means no planes ... I've got to get out, my psyche slipping. Get a ship to China, to the Berring Strait? ... Get my bearings straight on a loose head ... Only image left is a nightmare of wounded motorbikes mauled by children playing soldiers —

They're yelling, DILI HAS FALLEN!'

Cheap Flight Gone

On the fifth floor of the general's grand motel Lennie nervously explains the tickets loss to The Shelf. He's unimpressed and walks around the room sideways inti-midating Lennie. Below the manager arthritic, holds the pistol, "very excited".

Lennie is laughing out of control. Seeing fire on the instrument panel he checks the open runway before taking flight —The front door — but Tony lands too close. Pupils tearing at Lennie in the doorway, manifolding arms. He strangles Lennie, who is amazed, reeling around the room. Lockstep, a dancing nightmare — There are calls of 'Lousy Motorbike' and 'Cheap Flight Gone!'

Lennie leaves the window at an awkward angle.

His mouth open, four fingers raised ...

Tony is calling, 'Goodbyyyyye!'

Lennie hits a new Yamaha. His body laid back over the bitumen undergoing change. Harassed students tear at his clothing. Slowly he raises four fingers in auto-suggestion. Green jungle uniforms come running, cradling submachine guns —

Overhead, the last flight gone.

BALI ONE

BALI ONE

On Mount Batur overlooking Trunyan's open cemetries. Bodies stinking in the air. Their spirits departing. In the losmen eating fried fish spiced with death-ray, Sam feels cold weather coming on ... Down below, a skiff sets sail. Donna sick of the long haul wants to get on her own way south. She wants Sam to take her, care for her, be a brother. She wants to stay pure, purify herself; she doesn't want to make love — 'Love is already made,' she says.

Sitting in their bare room on the floor between single beds in a heap of blankets. The mountain cold drags bodies together.

Sam eats an orange, green skin sun-drenched inside. He unwinds one continuous parabola and lets it drop to the floor. Collects his things. Behind the losmen, trucks roar up the pass. Paying for his food he prepares to leave the plateau. She follows him in the light rain, the road winding blue against lush-green. She slumps under a rocky overhang, Sam in a poncho on the road.

Exhaust fumes on the corner. Natives pass with huge cane baskets sprouting from their heads, Sam smoking in the rain. Hailing a truck they scramble in, sucking rambutans.

Afternoon light drains terraced rice fields and Balinese in white shirts herd buffalos towards a distant village. Grey streaks in the sky and orange fires, rain falling in the back of the truck. Clove smoke strewn over coloured blouses and a dozen khaki uniforms.

BALI
TOO

BALI TOO

North to Singaraja, land of the belly banana — Dutch port with cinemas showing ROCKY HORROR — A DIFFERENT SET OF JAWS. Donkeys hobble aching taxis through streets smelling of durian. Their truck stops in the neon central square. One-eyed street-sellers laugh at their wet locks ...

— Muslim Town —

A hot night. Crisp sheets. Sam not sleeping . . . She pines for home, lighting another mosquito coil. Sam surveys the space between their beds, — 'What are we doing, here?' he says.

—Muslims throw stones—

On Lovina Beach, like two infants they lay together on the gravel shore. Sea washes; there's no surf. Not blue in the sun. Hermit crabs scuttle up the beach as fishermen drag their nets through the sea ... On an orange towel she pretends sleep so that Sam will forget her nakedness.

—Muslims stone dogs—

Heated ceremonies. He tries to appease her offering everything. Her life controls his and his shape begins to disappear. Her voice keeps him away. Sitting on his bed, still, separate. Their room becomes a cave lit by a single lamp. Bodies a decomposing Paradise / sex, some way out —

'Sam you're desperate,' she says.

'I'm desperate!'

'Yes.'

'I can't bear you cutting off. Your feelings — '

'You're fixed, in the head.'

Winding the sheets.

'You're just as fixed.'

She remakes the bed then sits up in one corner —

'We're opposites,' her fingers crossed.

'Well you take the North Pole and I'll take the South Pole... '

'Har-bloody-har.'

She holds him. Wounded. Feeling indented gravel marks from tiny stones they paw each other's fear, bodies dismantled on the bed. Outside the noise increases and the windows rattle. The fan whines. Like two monkeys they pick at each other under a dreadful umbrella.

SOLO

SOLO

Salo.

The beginning of the market night. Smell of tufu and bananas burning under pink late afternoon. Toothless hags embrace beautiful children stalking their way home. Carts rub the street. Pale light of Java the flat land, of rice fields and stooped swinging bodies.

Sam walks through the market amongst the dark skins. Eyes. All smiling at his body, blue thongs clipping the market place.

Mosque-call at dusk. The custom leaving. Over the walls of the Kraton palace an aching religious wail. One voice calling to the mass, the market emptying. Stalls drain to empty trinkets.

Towards the palace and its walled maze, the ancient city now sprawled out, left origin —

Selamat tidur

Solo rising from the corpse of a Sultan's past. Sam in the city-stream through crazy traffic *Sola Salo Salo SOLO!* —youth-mouth hanging out, bus passing— Old ones blind slumped over hot susu stands hearing the dusk in. Asleep in the corpse of the day — Solo — City of aloneness. Lost among thousands, millions stretching over rice fields, one single green horizon —thin strips of banana leaf fly as protective spirits on the green line— Youths strut on individual comers, scorched in the heat.

— Labyrinthian city of flared kereosene —

He wanders the streets looking for the wall, the way home to the hotel. Short cuts. In the dark he stands waiting for directions. Into Pasar Malam, night market; blazing alleyways of laughing Javanese following*his trail. Their life-dreams of humming clove cigarettes and soft drinks. Rice boiling in the night mass —Each single man— with black fez, sharp face, agile frame; eating cooked chicken torn apart. Delicate fingers move to a hundred mouths ...

Swirling bejaks and child choruses follow him through the lanes.

Dimana ada jalan Kratonan?

Kota Hotel?

Orphans in the street stare or chant wildly, *Bodoh fakir, bodoh fakir.* Through crowded night lanes the bejaks follow seeking fare.

Sam finds the wall. He holds the wall. Chest to stone his cheek on rough brick, he reads JALAN KRATONAN. Turning into a small lane he stops confused. Candles mark the house fronts, the many faces —

Dimana ada ? . . . Kota Hotel?

In blackness, just a body in space. Solo. Walking down the lane—
'I've lost my language.'

He finds a squatting figure beneath two lamps by the wall. He wakes the monkey man —flash of an ice-cream seller in the hot sun— he turns right, knowing destination, —

Sudden music. Neon.

A wedding departs from their hotel. Reels of black fez. Cummerbands, each holding an elaborate keris. Mottled fabrics and frangipani, image — mardigras. Spiced meats and sweet fruits held in the air —

Caught in the crowd, the party moving on — Above him, shining KOTA HOTEL, and singing from the street '*Sala-Salo-Solo ... '*

BALI HAI

BALI HAI

On the island, Lake Bedugal losmen by the blue. Old volcanoes crowned with bananas and sweet corn. Mist drifts over the frozen lake ... Sam alone in a deserted hotel scribbles a letter to Donna in Java. Skiffs calm-distant on the line. Sliced morning air ... writing to her over bamboo, grinding distillation from a deep recess —

Empty. Silence. In repose. There's no resistance now. I'm sitting easily on sloping wood and half of me is floating somewhere over the lake. You've taken some part of me away, a temporary loss. There's no other travellers here. I don't see the staff yet find the room in order and a skiff moored for me outside the hotel. I leave them a little money. Children coax me into the fishing boat, this happens every day. This place tears down all the mental screens.

By the lake, old bamboo losmens withering under the intense heat. Buckling noises splinter each sharp blue day. Sam sits drinking in an arena of dilapidated chairs and tables, weather-soaked; his arms fall resting to his sides. Postcards litter the faded table-top. He looks at the views, his lines to her —

SINGAPORE THE LION CITY

Thousands moved here from the open countryside. Now they tear down the Malay villages for multi-storied office blocks. The city smoulders as a house of the head. Bodies buffet android across the landscape. You were right, all cities are the same. So was Heironymous Bosch.

TEMPLE BY THE SHORES OF LAKE BEDUGAL

In this temple a young man gave me a scarf. His red scarf around my waist allowed me into new space. I walked with a continual sky of old volcanoes, unafraid. An older man and his son were fishing by the water under a huge umbrella. Light rain ... Two small fish shone near their feet. Walking amongst the many tiered and sacred images —

MONKEY DANCE AT KUTA BEACH

Wide-eyed youths wailing Ketjack dance a hundred on two sides — force/relent. Centre-stage a couple embrace, their supple lines. When he leaves, Rangda enters, enticing the woman. From each side hundreds of fingers call, then backwards into darkness. The husband enters and the woman storms confusion, a mad dance begins. The forces of chaos & co-operation magnify from their partnership into an infinity of forms through the wailing youths — tjak-tjak-tjak- tjak.

The manager's children beckon to him from their moored canoe. He gets in and helps them paddle into deeper water. Its blue and yellow rigging slides across the lake. In the volcanoes shadow they talk remnants of two languages. On shore, red scarves and a black umbrella dot the luminous green. The peeling facade of bamboo hotels ...

Drifting, Sam sees reflections of himself. The children talk of travelling and he wants to move on. Smoke seems to rise from their hotel. Sam tells them it is his postcards burning down.

ACKNOWLEDGEMENTS

The author would like to thank the Literature Board of the Australia Council for the Arts for generous assistance through half-fellowships taken up in 1976 & 1977.

Earlier versions of these stories appeared in *Another One for Mary, Aspect, Bananas, Contempa, Dodo*, Honi Soit, *Leatherjacket, Muese, Opus, Predator of the Marvellous, Riverrun, Tabloid Story* & *Westerly*. Several were read over Writer's radio 5UV & 3CR, prior to publication.

In the Gas Oven was anthologised in Michael Butterworth's *Savoy Dreams* (Savoy Books UK 1984)

Four lines from Charles Olsen's 'Maximus Poems Volume Three' (Grossman, 1975) & two lines from Henry Miller's 'Tropic of Cancer'.

Notes on the text:
The Enticer — the Sydney Harbour Bridge was built to the same design as the Hell Gate Bridge, New York.
Scar City — The house in Palmer Street was number 212. Anna Kavan wrote 'A Scarcity of Love'.
At the Raffles Hotel — written in the Palace Hotel, Singapore, to the tune of a motorcycle repair shop downstairs.
Layback Lennie — written in a Legian restaurant, Bali, on a rented typewriter during Timor Intervention, December 1975.
Bali One — The Kintamani Hotel. In October 1974, Andrew Peacock's Bali speech declared that there would be a change of government in Australia. I heard this fact at the Papua New Guinea Embassy on October 21 1974. Three weeks later, at this hotel, Peacock's dream became true.
Bali Two — The Merta Yadna, Singaraja & Losman Manggala, Lovina Beach.
Solo — Surakarta, central Java, the Kota Hotel.
Bali Hai — The Hotel Bedugal.

Printed in Australia
AUHW020834250222
360132AU00004B/20